I0535231

Sara Teasdale – Young Love & Other Poems

Poetry is a fascinating use of language. With almost a million words at its command it is not surprising that these Isles have produced some of the most beautiful, moving and descriptive verse through the centuries. In this series we look at individual poets who have shaped and influenced their craft and cement their place in our heritage. In this volume we look at the works of Sara Teasdale.

Sara Trevor Teasdale was born on August 8, 1884 in St Louis, Missouri. A woman of poor health it was only at 14 that she was well enough to begin school. Her education finished in 1903 at Hosmer Hall and her first poetry publication was in 1907 with her second book in 1911.

She was courted by various men among them Vachel Lindsay, a great poet but one who thought he could not provide a suitable standard of living for Sara so she married Ernst Filsinger in 1914. Sara's third poetry collection, Rivers to the Sea, was published in 1915 and was a best seller, being reprinted many times. A year later, in 1916 the married couple moved to New York City.

In 1917 she released the poetry collection Love Songs and the following year it won three awards: the Columbia University Poetry Society prize, the 1918 Pulitzer Prize for poetry and the annual prize of the Poetry Society of America.

By 1929 Sara was deeply unhappy and lonely so she moved interstate for three months, in order to gain a divorce. She did not wish to inform Filsinger, and only at the insistence of her lawyers as the divorce was going through did she - Filsinger was shocked and surprised.

After her divorce Sara remained in New York City and resumed her friendship with Vachel Lindsay, who was by this time married with children.

1931 Vachel Lindsay committed suicide. Two year later Sara to was dead - overdosing on sleeping pills. She is buried in the Bellefontaine Cemetery in St. Louis.

Many samples of our audiobooks are at our youtube channel http://www.youtube.com/user/PortablePoetry?feature=mhee   Complete volumes on many poets, themes and our other products can be purchased from iTunes, Amazon and other digital stores

Index Of Titles

A Cry

Oh, there are eyes that he can see,
And hands to make his hands rejoice,
But to my lover I must be
Only a voice.

Oh, there are breasts to bear his head,
And lips whereon his lips can lie,
But I must be till I am dead
Only a cry.

A Winter Night

My window-pane is starred with frost,
The world is bitter cold to-night,
The moon is cruel, and the wind
Is like a two-edged sword to smite.

God pity all the homeless ones,
The beggars pacing to and fro,
God pity all the poor to-night
Who walk the lamp-lit streets of snow.

My room is like a bit of June,
Warm and close-curtained fold on fold,
But somewhere, like a homeless child,
My heart is crying in the cold.

Alone

I am alone, in spite of love,
In spite of all I take and give
In spite of all your tenderness,
Sometimes I am not glad to live.

I am alone, as though I stood
On the highest peak of the tired gray world,
About me only swirling snow,
Above me, endless space unfurled;

With earth hidden and heaven hidden,
And only my own spirit's pride
To keep me from the peace of those
Who are not lonely, having died.

At Midnight
Now at last I have come to see what life is,
Nothing is ever ended, everything only begun,
And the brave victories that seem so splendid
Are never really won.

Even love that I built my spirit's house for,
Comes like a brooding and a baffled guest,
And music and men's praise and even laughter
Are not so good as rest.

At Sea
In the pull of the wind I stand, lonely,
On the deck of a ship, rising, falling,
Wild night around me, wild water under me,
Whipped by the storm, screaming and calling.

Earth is hostile and the sea hostile,
Why do I look for a place to rest?
I must fight always and die fighting
With fear an unhealing wound in my breast.

Barter
Life has loveliness to sell,
All beautiful and splendid things,
Blue waves whitened on a cliff,
Soaring fire that sways and sings,
And children's faces looking up
Holding wonder like a cup.

Life has loveliness to sell,
Music like a curve of gold,
Scent of pine trees in the rain,
Eyes that love you, arms that hold,
And for your spirit's still delight,
Holy thoughts that star the night.

Spend all you have for loveliness,
Buy it and never count the cost;
For one white singing hour of peace
Count many a year of strife well lost,
And for a breath of ecstasy
Give all you have been, or could be.

Buried Love

I have come to bury Love
Beneath a tree,
In the forest tall and black
Where none can see.

I shall put no flowers at his head,
Nor stone at his feet,
For the mouth I loved so much
Was bittersweet.

I shall go no more to his grave,
For the woods are cold.
I shall gather as much of joy
As my hands can hold.

I shall stay all day in the sun
Where the wide winds blow,
But oh, I shall cry at night
When none will know.

Change

Remember me as I was then;
Turn from me now, but always see
The laughing shadowy girl who stood
At midnight by the flowering tree,
With eyes that love had made as bright
As the trembling stars of the summer night.

Turn from me now, but always hear
The muted laughter in the dew
Of that one year of youth we had,
The only youth we ever knew
Turn from me now, or you will see
What other years have done to me.

Compensation

I should be glad of loneliness
And hours that go on broken wings,
A thirsty body, a tired heart
And the unchanging ache of things,

If I could make a single song
As lovely and as full of light,

As hushed and brief as a falling star
On a winter night.

Debt

What do I owe to you
Who loved me deep and long?
You never gave my spirit wings
Or gave my heart a song.

But oh, to him I loved,
Who loved me not at all,
I owe the open gate
That led through heaven's wall.

Doubt

My soul lives in my body's house,
And you have both the house and her
But sometimes she is less your own
Than a wild, gay adventurer;
A restless and an eager wraith,
How can I tell what she will do
Oh, I am sure of my body's faith,
But what if my soul broke faith with you?

Dusk In War Time

A half-hour more and you will lean
To gather me close in the old sweet way
But oh, to the woman over the sea
Who will come at the close of day?

A half-hour more and I will hear
The key in the latch and the strong, quick tread
But oh, the woman over the sea
Waiting at dusk for one who is dead!

Dust

When I went to look at what had long been hidden,
A jewel laid long ago in a secret place,
I trembled, for I thought to see its dark deep fire
But only a pinch of dust blew up in my face.

I almost gave my life long ago for a thing
That has gone to dust now, stinging my eyes

It is strange how often a heart must be broken
Before the years can make it wise.

Embers

I said, "My youth is gone
Like a fire beaten out by the rain,
That will never sway and sing
Or play with the wind again."

I said, "It is no great sorrow
That quenched my youth in me,
But only little sorrows
Beating ceaselessly."

I thought my youth was gone,
But you returned
Like a flame at the call of the wind
It leaped and burned;

Threw off its ashen cloak,
And gowned anew
Gave itself like a bride
Once more to you.

Faces

People that I meet and pass
In the city's broken roar,
Faces that I lose so soon
And have never found before,

Do you know how much you tell
In the meeting of our eyes,
How ashamed I am, and sad
To have pierced your poor disguise?

Secrets rushing without sound
Crying from your hiding places
Let me go, I cannot bear
The sorrow of the passing faces.

People in the restless street,
Can it be, oh can it be
In the meeting of our eyes
That you know as much of me?

Four Winds

"Four winds blowing through the sky,
You have seen poor maidens die,
Tell me then what I shall do
That my lover may be true."
Said the wind from out the south,
"Lay no kiss upon his mouth,"
And the wind from out the west,
"Wound the heart within his breast,"
And the wind from out the east,
"Send him empty from the feast,"
And the wind from out the north,
"In the tempest thrust him forth;
When thou art more cruel than he,
Then will Love be kind to thee."

Gifts

I gave my first love laughter,
I gave my second tears,
I gave my third love silence
Through all the years.

My first love gave me singing,
My second eyes to see,
But oh, it was my third love
Who gave my soul to me.

Houses Of Dreams

You took my empty dreams
And filled them every one
With tenderness and nobleness,
April and the sun.

The old empty dreams
Where my thoughts would throng
Are far too full of happiness
To even hold a song.

Oh, the empty dreams were dim
And the empty dreams were wide,
They were sweet and shadowy houses
Where my thoughts could hide.

But you took my dreams away

And you made them all come true
My thoughts have no place now to play,
And nothing now to do.

If Death Is Kind

Perhaps if Death is kind, and there can be returning,
We will come back to earth some fragrant night,
And take these lanes to find the sea, and bending
Breathe the same honeysuckle, low and white.

We will come down at night to these resounding beaches
And the long gentle thunder of the sea,
Here for a single hour in the wide starlight
We shall be happy, for the dead are free.

In A Garden

The world is resting without sound or motion,
Behind the apple tree the sun goes down
Painting with fire the spires and the windows
In the elm-shaded town.

Beyond the calm Connecticut the hills lie
Silvered with haze as fruits still fresh with bloom,
The swallows weave in flight across the zenith
On an aerial loom.

Into the garden peace comes back with twilight,
Peace that since noon had left the purple phlox,
The heavy-headed asters, the late roses
And swaying hollyhocks.

For at high-noon I heard from this same garden
The far-off murmur as when many come;
Up from the village surged the blind and beating
Red music of a drum;

And the hysterical sharp fife that shattered
The brittle autumn air,
While they came, the young men marching
Past the village square. . . .

Across the calm Connecticut the hills change
To violet, the veils of dusk are deep
Earth takes her children's many sorrows calmly
And stills herself to sleep.

Let It Be Forgotten
Let it be forgotten, as a flower is forgotten,
Forgotten as a fire that once was singing gold.
Let it be forgotten forever and ever,
Time is a kind friend, he will make us old.

If anyone asks, say it was forgotten
Long and long ago,
As a flower, as a fire, as a hushed footfall
In a long-forgotten snow.

Moonlight
It will not hurt me when I am old,
A running tide where moonlight burned
Will not sting me like silver snakes;
The years will make me sad and cold,
It is the happy heart that breaks.

The heart asks more than life can give,
When that is learned, then all is learned;
The waves break fold on jewelled fold,
But beauty itself is fugitive,
It will not hurt me when I am old.

Open Windows
Out of the window a sea of green trees
Lift their soft boughs like the arms of a dancer,
They beckon and call me, "Come out in the sun!"
But I cannot answer.

I am alone with Weakness and Pain,
Sick abed and June is going,
I cannot keep her, she hurries by
With the silver-green of her garments blowing.

Men and women pass in the street
Glad of the shining sapphire weather,
But we know more of it than they,
Pain and I together.

They are the runners in the sun,
Breathless and blinded by the race,

But we are watchers in the shade
Who speak with Wonder face to face.

Pain
Waves are the sea's white daughters,
And raindrops the children of rain,
But why for my shimmering body
Have I a mother like Pain?

Night is the mother of stars,
And wind the mother of foam
The world is brimming with beauty,
But I must stay at home.

Riches
I have no riches but my thoughts,
Yet these are wealth enough for me;
My thoughts of you are golden coins
Stamped in the mint of memory;

And I must spend them all in song,
For thoughts, as well as gold, must be
Left on the hither side of death
To gain their immortality.

Sleepless
If I could have your arms tonight-
But half the world and the broken sea
Lie between you and me.

The autumn rain reverberates in the courtyard,
Beating all night against the barren stone,
The sound of useless rain in the desolate courtyard
Makes me more alone.

If you were here, if you were only here
My blood cries out to you all night in vain
As sleepless as the rain.

Snowfall
"She can't be unhappy," you said,
"The smiles are like stars in her eyes,
And her laugh is thistledown

Around her low replies."
"Is she unhappy?" you said
But who has ever known
Another's heartbreak
All he can know is his own;
And she seems hushed to me,
As hushed as though
Her heart were a hunter's fire
Smothered in snow.

Spring Rain
I thought I had forgotten,
But it all came back again
To-night with the first spring thunder
In a rush of rain.

I remembered a darkened doorway
Where we stood while the storm swept by,
Thunder gripping the earth
And lightning scrawled on the sky.

The passing motor busses swayed,
For the street was a river of rain,
Lashed into little golden waves
In the lamp light's stain.

With the wild spring rain and thunder
My heart was wild and gay;
Your eyes said more to me that night
Than your lips would ever say. . . .

I thought I had forgotten,
But it all came back again
To-night with the first spring thunder
In a rush of rain.

Stars
Alone in the night
On a dark hill
With pines around me
Spicy and still,

And a heaven full of stars
Over my head,
White and topaz

And misty red;

Myriads with beating
Hearts of fire
That aeons
Cannot vex or tire;

Up the dome of heaven
Like a great hill,
I watch them marching
Stately and still,
And I know that I
Am honored to be
Witness
Of so much majesty.

The Coin
Into my heart's treasury
I slipped a coin
That time cannot take
Nor a thief purloin,

Oh better than the minting
Of a gold-crowned king
Is the safe-kept memory
Of a lovely thing.

The Ghost
I went back to the clanging city,
I went back where my old loves stayed,
But my heart was full of my new love's glory,
My eyes were laughing and unafraid.

I met one who had loved me madly
And told his love for all to hear
But we talked of a thousand things together,
The past was buried too deep to fear.

I met the other, whose love was given
With never a kiss and scarcely a word
Oh, it was then the terror took me
Of words unuttered that breathed and stirred.

Oh, love that lives its life with laughter
Or love that lives its life with tears

Can die - but love that is never spoken
Goes like a ghost through the winding years. . . .

I went back to the clanging city,
I went back where my old loves stayed,
My heart was full of my new love's glory,
But my eyes were suddenly afraid.

The Lamp

If I can bear your love like a lamp before me,
When I go down the long steep Road of Darkness,
I shall not fear the everlasting shadows,
Nor cry in terror.

If I can find out God, then I shall find Him,
If none can find Him, then I shall sleep soundly,
Knowing how well on earth your love sufficed me,
A lamp in darkness.

The Mystery

Your eyes drink of me,
Love makes them shine,
Your eyes that lean
So close to mine.

We have long been lovers,
We know the range
Of each other's moods
And how they change;

But when we look
At each other so
Then we feel
How little we know;

The spirit eludes us,
Timid and free
Can I ever know you
Or you know me?

The Return

He has come, he is here,
My love has come home,
The minutes are lighter

Than flying foam,

The hours are like dancers
On gold-slippered feet,
The days are young runners
Naked and fleet

For my love has returned,
He is home, he is here,
In the whole world no other
Is dear as my dear!

The Sanctuary
If I could keep my innermost Me
Fearless, aloof and free
Of the least breath of love or hate,
And not disconsolate
At the sick load of sorrow laid on men;
If I could keep a sanctuary there
Free even of prayer,
If I could do this, then,
With quiet candor as I grew more wise
I could look even at God with grave forgiving eyes.

The Treasure
When they see my songs
They will sigh and say,
"Poor soul, wistful soul,
Lonely night and day."

They will never know
All your love for me
Surer than the spring,
Stronger than the sea;

Hidden out of sight
Like a miser's gold
In forsaken fields
Where the wind is cold.

The Voice
Atoms as old as stars,
Mutation on mutation,
Millions and millions of cells

Dividing yet still the same,
From air and changing earth,
From ancient Eastern rivers,
From turquoise tropic seas,
Unto myself I came.

My spirit like my flesh
Sprang from a thousand sources,
From cave-man, hunter and shepherd,
From Karnak, Cyprus, Rome;

The living thoughts in me
Spring from dead men and women,
Forgotten time out of mind
And many as bubbles of foam.

Here for a moment's space
Into the light out of darkness,
I come and they come with me
Finding words with my breath;

From the wisdom of many life-times
Seek for Beauty, she only
Fights with man against Death!"

The Wanderer
I saw the sunset-colored sands,
The Nile like flowing fire between,
Where Rameses stares forth serene,
And Ammon's heavy temple stands.

I saw the rocks where long ago,
Above the sea that cries and breaks,
Swift Perseus with Medusa's snakes
Set free the maiden white like snow.

And many skies have covered me,
And many winds have blown me forth,
And I have loved the green, bright north,
And I have loved the cold, sweet sea.

But what to me are north and south,
And what the lure of many lands,
Since you have leaned to catch my hands
And lay a kiss upon my mouth.

The Years

To-night I close my eyes and see
A strange procession passing me
The years before I saw your face
Go by me with a wistful grace;
They pass, the sensitive, shy years,
As one who strives to dance, half blind with tears.

The years went by and never knew
That each one brought me nearer you;
Their path was narrow and apart
And yet it led me to your heart
Oh, sensitive, shy years, oh, lonely years,
That strove to sing with voices drowned in tears.

Understanding

I understood the rest too well,
And all their thoughts have come to be
Clear as grey sea-weed in the swell
Of a sunny shallow sea.

But you I never understood,
Your spirit's secret hides like gold
Sunk in a Spanish galleon
Ages ago in waters cold.

White Fog

Heaven-invading hills are drowned
In wide moving waves of mist,
Phlox before my door are wound
In dripping wreaths of amethyst.

Ten feet away the solid earth
Changes into melting cloud,
There is a hush of pain and mirth,
No bird has heart to speak aloud.

Here in a world without a sky,
Without the ground, without the sea,
The one unchanging thing is I,
Myself remains to comfort me.

Arcturus

Arcturus brings the spring back
As surely now as when
He rose on eastern islands
For Grecian girls and men;

The twilight is as clear a blue,
The star as shaken and as bright,
And the same thought he gave to them
He gives to me to-night.

Because
Oh, because you never tried
To bow my will or break my pride,
And nothing of the cave-man made
You want to keep me half afraid,
Nor ever with a conquering air
You thought to draw me unaware
Take me, for I love you more
Than I ever loved before.

And since the body's maidenhood
Alone were neither rare nor good
Unless with it I gave to you
A spirit still untrammeled, too,
Take my dreams and take my mind
That were masterless as wind;
And "Master!" I shall say to you
Since you never asked me to.

Child, Child
Child, child, love while you can
The voice and the eyes and the soul of a man;
Never fear though it break your heart
Out of the wound new joy will start;
Only love proudly and gladly and well,
Though love be heaven or love be hell.

Child, child, love while you may,
For life is short as a happy day;
Never fear the thing you feel
Only by love is life made real;
Love, for the deadly sins are seven,
Only through love will you enter heaven.

Dew

As dew leaves the cobweb lightly
Threaded with stars,
Scattering jewels on the fence
And the pasture bars;
As dawn leaves the dry grass bright
And the tangled weeds
Bearing a rainbow gem
On each of their seeds;
So has your love, my lover,
Fresh as the dawn,
Made me a shining road
To travel on,
Set every common sight
Of tree or stone
Delicately alight
For me alone.

Driftwood

My forefathers gave me
My spirit's shaken flame,
The shape of hands, the beat of heart,
The letters of my name.

But it was my lovers,
And not my sleeping sires,
Who gave the flame its changeful
And iridescent fires;

As the driftwood burning
Learned its jewelled blaze
From the sea's blue splendor
Of colored nights and days.

Ebb Tide

When the long day goes by
And I do not see your face,
The old wild, restless sorrow
Steals from its hiding place.

My day is barren and broken,
Bereft of light and song,
A sea beach bleak and windy
That moans the whole day long.

To the empty beach at ebb tide,
Bare with its rocks and scars,
Come back like the sea with singing,
And light of a million stars.

Faults
They came to tell your faults to me,
They named them over one by one;
I laughed aloud when they were done,
I knew them all so well before,
Oh, they were blind, too blind to see
Your faults had made me love you more.

I Remembered
There never was a mood of mine,
Gay or heart-broken, luminous or dull,
But you could ease me of its fever
And give it back to me more beutiful.
In many another soul I broke the bread,
And drank the wine and played the happy guest,
But I was lonely, I remembered you;
The heart belong to him who knew it best.

I Thought Of You
I thought of you and how you love this beauty,
And walking up the long beach all alone
I heard the waves breaking in measured thunder
As you and I once heard their monotone.

Around me were the echoing dunes, beyond me
The cold and sparkling silver of the sea
We two will pass through death and ages lengthen
Before you hear that sound again with me.

In The End
All that could never be said,
All that could never be done,
Wait for us at last
Somewhere back of the sun;

All the heart broke to forego
Shall be ours without pain,
We shall take them as lightly as girls

Pluck flowers after rain.

And when they are ours in the end
Perhaps after all
The skies will not open for us
Nor heaven be there at our call.

Lights
When we come home at night and close the door,
Standing together in the shadowy room,
Safe in our own love and the gentle gloom,
Glad of familiar wall and chair and floor,

Glad to leave far below the clanging city;
Looking far downward to the glaring street
Gaudy with light, yet tired with many feet,
In both of us wells up a wordless pity;

Men have tried hard to put away the dark;
A million lighted windows brilliantly
Inlay with squares of gold the winter night,
But to us standing here there comes the stark
Sense of the lives behind each yellow light,
And not one wholly joyous, proud, or free.

Love And Death
Shall we, too, rise forgetful from our sleep,
And shall my soul that lies within your hand
Remember nothing, as the blowing sand
Forgets the palm where long blue shadows creep
When winds along the darkened desert sweep?

Or would it still remember, tho' it spanned
A thousand heavens, while the planets fanned
The vacant ether with their voices deep?
Soul of my soul, no word shall be forgot,
Nor yet alone, beloved, shall we see

The desolation of extinguished suns,
Nor fear the void wherethro' our planet runs,
For still together shall we go and not
Fare forth alone to front eternity.

Meadowlarks

In the silver light after a storm,
Under dripping boughs of bright new green,
I take the low path to hear the meadowlarks
Alone and high-hearted as if I were a queen.
What have I to fear in life or death
Who have known three things: the kiss in the night,
The white flying joy when a song is born,
And meadowlarks whistling in silver light.

Message
I heard a cry in the night,
A thousand miles it came,
Sharp as a flash of light,
My name, my name!

It was your voice I heard,
You waked and loved me so
I send you back this word,
I know, I know!

Old Tunes
As the waves of perfume, heliotrope, rose,
Float in the garden when no wind blows,
Come to us, go from us, whence no one knows;

So the old tunes float in my mind,
And go from me leaving no trace behind,
Like fragrance borne on the hush of the wind.

But in the instant the airs remain
I know the laughter and the pain
Of times that will not come again.

I try to catch at many a tune
Like petals of light fallen from the moon,
Broken and bright on a dark lagoon,

But they float away - for who can hold
Youth, or perfume or the moon's gold?

On The Dunes
If there is any life when death is over,
These tawny beaches will know much of me,
I shall come back, as constant and as changeful

As the unchanging, many-colored sea.

If life was small, if it has made me scornful,
Forgive me; I shall straighten like a flame
In the great calm of death, and if you want me
Stand on the sea-ward dunes and call my name.

Places
Places I love come back to me like music,
Hush me and heal me when I am very tired;
I see the oak woods at Saxton's flaming
In a flare of crimson by the frost newly fired;

And I am thirsty for the spring in the valley
As for a kiss ungiven and long desired.
I know a bright world of snowy hills at Boonton,
A blue and white dazzling light on everything one sees,

The ice-covered branches of the hemlocks sparkle
Bending low and tinkling in the sharp thin breeze,
And iridescent crystals fall and crackle on the snow-crust
With the winter sun drawing cold blue shadows from the trees.

Violet now, in veil on veil of evening
The hills across from Cromwell grow dreamy and far;
A wood-thrush is singing soft as a viol
In the heart of the hollow where the dark pools are;

The primrose has opened her pale yellow flowers
And heaven is lighting star after star.
Places I love come back to me like music
Mid-ocean, midnight, the waves buzz drowsily;

In the ship's deep churning the eerie phosphorescence
Is like the souls of people who were drowned at sea,
And I can hear a man's voice, speaking, hushed, insistent,
At midnight, in mid-ocean, hour on hour to me.

Redbirds
Redbirds, redbirds,
Long and long ago,
What a honey-call you had
In hills I used to know;

Redbud, buckberry,

Wild plum-tree
And proud river sweeping
Southward to the sea,

Brown and gold in the sun
Sparkling far below,
Trailing stately round her bluffs
Where the poplars grow

Redbirds, redbirds,
Are you singing still
As you sang one May day
On Saxton's Hill?

Spray
I knew you thought of me all night,
I knew, though you were far away;
I felt your love blow over me
As if a dark wind-riven sea
Drenched me with quivering spray.

There are so many ways to love
And each way has its own delight
Then be content to come to me
Only as spray the beating sea
Drives inland through the night.

Summer Storm
The panther wind
Leaps out of the night,
The snake of lightning
Is twisting and white,
The lion of thunder
Roars - and we
Sit still and content
Under a tree
We have met fate together
And love and pain,
Why should we fear
The wrath of the rain!

The Garden
My heart is a garden tired with autumn,
Heaped with bending asters and dahlias heavy and dark,

In the hazy sunshine, the garden remembers April,
The drench of rains and a snow-drop quick and clear as a spark;

Daffodils blowing in the cold wind of morning,
And golden tulips, goblets holding the rain
The garden will be hushed with snow, forgotten soon, forgotten
After the stillness, will spring come again?

The Long Hill
I must have passed the crest a while ago
And now I am going down
Strange to have crossed the crest and not to know,
But the brambles were always catching the hem of my gown.

All the morning I thought how proud I should be
To stand there straight as a queen,
Wrapped in the wind and the sun with the world under me
But the air was dull, there was little I could have seen.

It was nearly level along the beaten track
And the brambles caught in my gown
But it's no use now to think of turning back,
The rest of the way will be only going down.

The New Moon
Day, you have bruised and beaten me,
As rain beats down the bright, proud sea,
Beaten my body, bruised my soul,
Left me nothing lovely or whole

Yet I have wrested a gift from you,
Day that dies in dusky blue:
For suddenly over the factories
I saw a moon in the cloudy seas

A wisp of beauty all alone
In a world as hard and gray as stone
Oh who could be bitter and want to die
When a maiden moon wakes up in the sky?

The Storm
I thought of you when I was wakened
By a wind that made me glad and afraid
Of the rushing, pouring sound of the sea

That the great trees made.

One thought in my mind went over and over
While the darkness shook and the leaves were thinned
I thought it was you who had come to find me,
You were the wind.

The Tree
Oh to be free of myself,
With nothing left to remember,
To have my heart as bare
As a tree in December;

Resting, as a tree rests
After its leaves are gone,
Waiting no more for a rain at night
Nor for the red at dawn;

But still, oh so still
While the winds come and go,
With no more fear of the hard frost
Or the bright burden of snow;

And heedless, heedless
If anyone pass and see
On the white page of the sky
Its thin black tracery.

The Wind
A wind is blowing over my soul,
I hear it cry the whole night through
Is there no peace for me on earth
Except with you?

Alas, the wind has made me wise,
Over my naked soul it blew,
There is no peace for me on earth
Even with you.

Tides
Love in my heart was a fresh tide flowing
Where the starlike sea gulls soar;
The sun was keen and the foam was blowing
High on the rocky shore.

But now in the dusk the tide is turning,
Lower the sea gulls soar,
And the waves that rose in resistless yearning
Are broken forevermore.

Water Lilies
If you have forgotten water lilies floating
On a dark lake among mountains in the afternoon shade,
If you have forgotten their wet, sleepy fragrance,
Then you can return and not be afraid.

But if you remember, then turn away forever
To the plains and the prairies where pools are far apart,
There you will not come at dusk on closing water lilies,
And the shadow of mountains will not fall on your heart.

Union Square
With the man I love who loves me not,
I walked in the street-lamps' flare;
We watched the world go home that night
In a flood through Union Square.
I leaned to catch the words he said
That were light as a snowflake falling;
Ah well that he never leaned to hear
The words my heart was calling.
And on we walked and on we walked
Past the fiery lights of the picture shows
Where the girls with thirsty eyes go by
On the errand each man knows.
And on we walked and on we walked,
At the door at last we said good-bye;
I knew by his smile he had not heard
My heart's unuttered cry.
With the man I love who loves me not
I walked in the street-lamps' flare
But oh, the girls who can ask for love
In the lights of Union Square.

The Unseen
Death went up the hall
Unseen by every one,
Trailing twilight robes
Past the nurse and the nun.

He paused at every door
And listened to the breath
Of those who did not know
How near they were to Death.
Death went up the hall
Unseen by nurse and nun;
He passed by many a door
But he entered one.

The Wayfarer
Love entered in my heart one day,
A sad, unwelcome guest;
But when he begged that he might stay,
I let him wait and rest.
He broke my sleep with sorrowing,
And shook my dreams with tears,
And when my heart was fain to sing,
He stilled its joy with fears.
But now that he has gone his way,
I miss the old sweet pain,
And sometimes in the night I pray
That he may come again.

When Love Was Born
When Love was born I think he lay
Right warm on Venus' breast,
And whiles he smiled and whiles would play
And whiles would take his rest.
But always, folded out of sight,
The wings were growing strong
That were to bear him off in flight
Erelong, erelong.

Wild Asters
In the spring I asked the daisies
If his words were true,
And the clever little daisies
Always knew.
Now the fields are brown and barren,
Bitter autumn blows,
And of all the stupid asters
Not one knows.

The Wine

I cannot die, who drank delight
From the cup of the crescent moon,
And hungrily as men eat bread,
Loved the scented nights of June.
The rest may die - but is there not
Some shining strange escape for me
Who sought in Beauty the bright wine
Of immortality?

Winter Dusk

I watch the great clear twilight
Veiling the ice-bowed trees;
Their branches tinkle faintly
With crystal melodies.
The larches bend their silver
Over the hush of snow;
One star is lighted in the west,
Two in the zenith glow.
For a moment I have forgotten
Wars and women who mourn
I think of the mother who bore me
And thank her that I was born.

Winter Sun

There was a bush with scarlet berries,
And there were hemlocks heaped with snow,
With a sound like surf on long sea-beaches
They took the wind and let it go.
The hills were shining in their samite,
Fold after fold they flowed away;
"Let come what may," your eyes were saying,
"At least we two have had to-day."

Wood Song

I heard a wood thrush in the dusk
Twirl three notes and make a star
My heart that walked with bitterness
Came back from very far.
Three shining notes were all he had,
And yet they made a starry call
I caught life back against my breast
And kissed it, scars and all.

Young Love

I

I cannot heed the words they say,
The lights grow far away and dim,
Amid the laughing men and maids
My eyes unbidden seek for him.
I hope that when he smiles at me
He does not guess my joy and pain,
For if he did, he is too kind
To ever look my way again.

II

I have a secret in my heart
No ears have ever heard,
And still it sings there day by day
Most like a caged bird.
And when it beats against the bars,
I do not set it free,
For I am happier to know
It only sings for me.

III

I wrote his name along the beach,
I love the letters so.
Far up it seemed and out of reach,
For still the tide was low.
But oh, the sea came creeping up,
And washed the name away,
And on the sand where it had been
A bit of sea-grass lay.
A bit of sea-grass on the sand,
Dropped from a mermaid's hair
Ah, had she come to kiss his name
And leave a token there?

IV

What am I that he should love me,
He who stands so far above me,
What am I?
I am like a cowslip turning
Toward the sky,
Where a planet's golden burning
Breaks the cowslip's heart with yearning,
What am I that he should love me,
What am I?

V

O dreams that flock about my sleep,
I pray you bring my love to me,
And let me think I hear his voice
Again ring free.
And if you care to please me well,
And live to-morrow in my mind,
Let him who was so cold before,
To-night seem kind.

VI

I plucked a daisy in the fields,
And there beneath the sun
I let its silver petals fall
One after one.
I said, "He loves me, loves me not,"
And oh, my heart beat fast,
The flower was kind, it let me say
"He loves me," last.
I kissed the little leafless stem,
But oh, my poor heart knew
The words the flower had said to me,
They were not true.

VII

I sent my love a letter,
And if he loves me not,
He shall not find my love for him
In any line or dot.
But if he loves me truly,
He'll find it hidden deep,
As dawn gleams red thro' chilly clouds
To eyes awaked from sleep.

VIII

The world is cold and gray and wet,
And I am heavy-hearted, yet
When I am home and look to see
The place my letters wait for me,
If I should find ONE letter there,
I think I should not greatly care
If it were rainy or were fair,
For all the world would suddenly
Seem like a festival to me.

IX

I hid three words within my heart,
That longed to fly to him,
At dawn they woke me with a start,
They sang till day was dim.
And now at last I let them fly,
As little birds should do,
And he will know the first is "I",
The others "Love" and "You".

X
Across the twilight's violet
His curtained window glimmers gold;
Oh happy light that round my love
Can fold.
Oh happy book within his hand,
Oh happy page he glorifies,
Oh happy little word beneath
His eyes.
But oh, thrice happy, happy I
Who love him more than songs can tell,
For in the heaven of his heart
I dwell.

Youth And The Pilgrim
Gray pilgrim, you have journeyed far,
I pray you tell to me
Is there a land where Love is not,
By shore of any sea?
For I am weary of the god,
And I would flee from him
Tho' I must take a ship and go
Beyond the ocean's rim.
"I know a port where Love is not,
The ship is in your hand,
Then plunge your sword within your breast
And you will reach the land."

www.ingramcontent.com/pod-product-compliance
Lightning Source LLC
Chambersburg PA
CBHW061506170626
46811CB00004B/1626